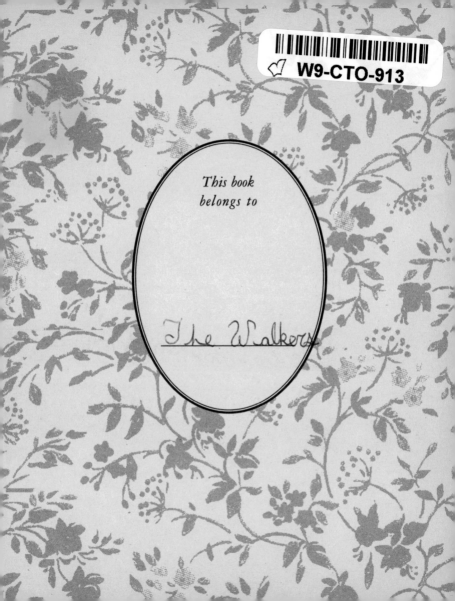

This book
belongs to

The Walkers

This Book Belongs to:

This Book Belongs to:

Anne of Green Gables

BY

L. M. MONTGOMERY

ADAPTED BY MARC D. FALKOFF

❖

▪ HARPERFESTIVAL®

A Division of HarperCollins*Publishers*

Anne of Green Gables was first published in 1908.

HarperCollins®, 📖®, and HarperFestival® are registered trademarks
of HarperCollins Publishers Inc.

Anne of Green Gables
Adaptation copyright © 1999 by HarperCollins Publishers Inc.

Library of Congress Cataloging-in-Publication Data
Montgomery, L. M. (Lucy Maud), 1874–1942.
  Anne of Green Gables / L.M. Montgomery ; adapted by Marc D. Falkoff.
    p.   cm.
  Summary: Anne, an eleven-year-old orphan, is sent by mistake to live with a
lonely, middle-aged brother and sister on a Prince Edward Island farm and proceeds
to make an indelible impression on everyone around her.
  ISBN 0-694-01284-X
  [1. Orphans—Fiction.   2. Friendship—Fiction.   3. Country life—Prince
Edward Island—Fiction.   4. Prince Edward Island—Fiction.]   I. Falkoff, Marc D.
II. Title.
PZ7.M768An   1999b   98-27873
[Fic]—DC21   CIP
                                                      AC

Typography by Fritz Metsch
1 2 3 4 5 6 7 8 9 10
❖
First Chapter Book Charmers edition, 1999

Visit us on the World Wide Web!
http://www.harperchildrens.com

CONTENTS

❖

Anne of Green Gables

Anne Arrives

❖

WHEN MATTHEW CUTHBERT arrived at the train station in his horse and buggy, he thought he was too early. There was no sign of the train, and no sign of the orphan boy he was to bring home to live with him and his sister at Green Gables Farm. The long platform was almost empty, and the only living creature in sight was a girl sitting on a pile of shingles. She was sitting there waiting for something or somebody, and since sitting and waiting was the only thing to do just then, she sat and waited with all her might.

Matthew tied his horse in the yard and went to ask the stationmaster if the train would soon be along.

"The train's been here and gone," the stationmaster answered. "But there was a passenger dropped off for you—a little girl. She's sitting out there on the shingles. I asked her to go into the ladies' waiting room, but she told me she wanted to stay outside. 'There was more scope for imagination outside,' she said."

"But I'm not expecting a girl," said Matthew. "It's a boy I've come for. Someone to help me work the farm. He should be here. He's coming from an orphanage in Nova Scotia."

"Guess there's some mistake," the stationmaster said. "I haven't got any more orphans hidden around here."

"I don't understand," said Matthew, wishing his sister Marilla were here to help.

"Well, you'd better ask the girl. I dare say she'll be able to explain—she's the talkingest girl I ever saw."

Matthew didn't know what to do, so he walked over to the girl sitting on the platform. This is what he saw: a child of about eleven, dressed in a very short, very tight, very ugly dress of thin yellowish cotton. She wore a brown sailor hat, and beneath the hat were two braids of very thick, very red hair. Her face was small, thin, and freckled. And she had large eyes that looked green in some lights and gray in others.

As soon as the girl saw that he was coming to her, she stood up, picked up her small bag, and held out her hand to him.

"I suppose you are Mr. Matthew Cuthbert of Green Gables?" she said in a clear, sweet voice. "I'm very glad to see you. I was beginning to be afraid you weren't coming for me, and I was imagining all the things that might have happened to prevent you. I had made up my mind that if you didn't come for me tonight I'd go down the track to that big wild cherry tree and climb up into it to stay all night. I wouldn't be a bit afraid, and it would be lovely to sleep in a wild cherry tree in the moonshine, don't you think? And I was quite sure you would come for me in the morning, if you didn't tonight."

Matthew took the little hand in his and decided what to do. He could not tell this child that there had been a mistake, so he would take her home and let Marilla do that.

"I'm sorry I was late," he said shyly. "Come along. The horse is over in the yard. Give me your bag."

"Oh, I can carry it," the child responded cheerfully. "It isn't heavy. I've got all my worldly goods in it, but it isn't heavy. Oh, I'm very glad you've come, even if it would have been nice to sleep in a wild cherry tree. We've got to drive a long piece, haven't we? I'm glad, because I love driving. Oh, it seems so wonderful that I'm going to live with you and belong to you. I've never belonged to anybody—not really. But the orphanage was the worst. I've only been in it four months, but that was enough. I don't suppose you ever were an orphan, so you can't possibly understand what it is like. It's worse than anything you could imagine. There is so little scope for the imagination in an orphanage. I used to lie awake at nights and imagine things, because I didn't have time in the day. I guess that's why I'm so thin—I *am* dreadful thin, aren't I? I'm all skin and bones. I do love to imagine I'm nice and plump, with dimples in my elbows."

With this, the girl stopped talking, partly because she was out of breath and partly because they had reached the buggy.

She didn't say anything else until they were rolling along the road, when suddenly she piped up again. "Oh, there are so many cherry trees all in bloom! This island is the bloomiest place. I just love it already, and I'm so glad I'm going to live here. I've always heard that Prince Edward Island is the prettiest place in the world, and I used to imagine I was living here, but I never really expected I would. It's delightful when your imaginations come true, isn't it? But these red roads are so funny. What makes the roads red?"

"Well, now, I dunno," said Matthew, shaking his head and grinning.

"Well, that is one of the things to find out sometime. Isn't it splendid to think of all the things there are to find out about? It just makes me feel glad to be alive— it's such an interesting world. It wouldn't be half so interesting if we knew all about everything, would it? There'd be no scope for imagination then, would there? But am I talking too much? People are always telling me I do. Would you rather I didn't talk? If you say so, I'll stop. I *can* stop when I make up my mind to it, although it's difficult."

Matthew, however, was enjoying himself. He kind of liked her chatter. So he said, "Oh, you can talk as much as you like. I don't mind."

"Oh, I'm so glad. I know you and I are going to get along together fine. It's such a relief to talk when one wants to and not be told that children should be seen and not heard. I've had that said to me a million times if I have once. And people laugh at me because I use big words. But if you have big ideas, you have to use big words to express them, don't you?"

"Well, now, that seems reasonable," said Matthew.

"Is there a brook anywhere near Green Gables?"

"Well, yes, there's one right below the house."

"Fancy! It's always been one of my dreams to live near a brook. I never expected I would, though. Dreams don't often come true, do they? Wouldn't it be nice if they did? But just now I feel pretty nearly perfectly happy. I can't feel *exactly* perfectly happy because—well, what color would you call this?"

She held up a braid of her hair before Matthew's eyes.

"It's red, isn't it?" he said.

The girl let the braid drop back with a sigh that seemed to come from her very toes.

"Yes, it's red," she said sadly. "Now you see why I can't be perfectly happy. Nobody could who has red hair. I don't mind the other things so much—the freckles and the green eyes and my skinniness. I can imagine them away. But I *cannot* imagine that red hair away. Which would you rather be if you had the choice—divinely beautiful or angelically good?"

"Well, now, I—I don't know exactly." Matthew felt a little dizzy listening to this girl.

"Neither do I. I can never decide. But it doesn't make much real difference, for it isn't likely I'll ever be either. It's certain I'll never be angelically good."

When they had driven up the further hill and around a corner, Matthew said, "We're pretty near home now. That's Green Gables over there."

"Oh, Mr. Cuthbert! It seems as if I must be in a dream. Do you know, my arm must be black and blue from the elbow up, for I've pinched myself so many times today. It's lovely—so lovely!"

Matthew shifted in his seat. He felt glad that it would be Marilla who would have to tell this strange little girl that Green Gables would not be her home after all.

[2]

Anne Meets Marilla

❖

MARILLA CAME TO the door when she heard Matthew's horse. But when she saw the little girl with the long braids of red hair, she stopped short.

"Matthew Cuthbert, who's that?" she cried. "Where is the boy?"

"There wasn't any boy. There was only her." He nodded at the child, remembering that he had never even asked her name.

"No boy! But there *must* have been a boy," said Marilla. "We sent word to bring a boy."

"Well, they brought *her*. I asked the stationmaster. And I had to bring her home. She couldn't be left at the station."

"Well, this is a pretty piece of business!" cried Marilla.

During this discussion the child began to grow pale. Suddenly she understood.

"You don't want me!" she cried. "You don't want me because I'm not a boy! I might have expected it. Nobody ever did want me. I might have known it was all too beautiful to last. I might have known nobody really did want me. Oh, what shall I do? I'm going to burst into tears!"

And that's just what she did. Marilla and Matthew looked at each other, but neither of them knew what to say or do. Finally Marilla said, "Well, well, there's no need to cry so about it."

"Yes, there *is* need! *You* would cry, too, if you were an orphan and had come to a place you thought was going to be home and found that they didn't want you because you weren't a boy. Oh, this is the most *tragical* thing that ever happened to me!"

Marilla almost smiled at the girl's "tragical" speech.

"Well, don't cry anymore. We're not going to turn you out of doors tonight. What's your name?"

The child hesitated for a moment.

"Will you please call me Cordelia?" she said eagerly.

"*Call* you Cordelia! Is that your name?"

"No-o-o, it's not exactly my name, but I would love to be called Cordelia. It's such a perfectly elegant name."

"I don't know what on earth you mean. If Cordelia isn't your name, what is?"

"Anne Shirley. But, oh, please do call me Cordelia. It can't matter much to you what you call me if I'm only going to be here a little while, can it? And Anne is such an unromantic name."

"Unromantic, fiddlesticks!" said Marilla. "Anne is a real good sensible name. You've no need to be ashamed of it."

"Oh, I'm not ashamed of it," said Anne, "only I like Cordelia better. I've always imagined that my name was Cordelia. But if you call me Anne, please call me Anne spelled with an *e*."

"What difference does it make how it's spelled?" asked Marilla, trying again not to smile.

"Oh, it makes *such* a difference. It *looks* so much nicer. When you hear a name pronounced, can't you always see it in your mind, just as if it was printed out? I can, and *A-n-n* looks dreadful, but *A-n-n-e* looks so much nicer."

"Very well, then, Anne-spelled-with-an-*e*, can you tell us how this mistake came to be made? We sent word to the orphanage to send us a boy. Weren't there any boys there?"

"Oh, yes, there were loads of them. But the matron said *distinctly* that you wanted a girl about eleven years old. And she thought I would do. You don't know how delighted I was. I couldn't sleep all last night for joy. Oh, if I was very beautiful and had nut-brown hair, would you keep me?"

"No. We want a boy to help Matthew on the farm. A girl would be of no use to us. Now go wash up and come to supper."

Anne did as she was told, and they sat down to supper. But Anne could not eat.

"You're not eating anything," said Marilla.

"I can't. I'm in the depths of despair. Can you eat when you are in the depths of despair?"

"I've never been in the depths of despair, so I can't say," responded Marilla.

"Weren't you? Well, did you ever try to *imagine* you were in the depths of despair?"

"No, I didn't."

"Then I don't think you can understand what it's like. It's a very uncomfortable feeling indeed. When you try to eat, a lump comes right up in your throat and you can't swallow anything, not even if it was a chocolate caramel. I had one chocolate caramel once two years ago, and it was simply delicious. I've often dreamed since then that I had a lot of chocolate caramels, but I always wake up just when I'm going to eat them. I do hope you won't be offended because I can't eat. Everything is extremely nice, but still I cannot eat."

"I guess she's tired," said Matthew. "Best put her to bed, Marilla."

She brought Anne up to the spare room, made sure she had a nightgown, and settled her into bed. Anne scrunched up and pulled the comforter over her head.

"Good night," said Marilla.

Anne's white face and big eyes appeared suddenly from under the covers.

"How can you call it a *good* night when you know it must be the very worst night I've ever had?" she said. Then she dived down into the covers again.

Marilla went slowly down to the kitchen and began to wash the supper dishes. "Well, this is a pretty kettle of fish," she said to her brother. "She'll have to be sent back to the orphanage."

"Yes, I suppose so," said Matthew.

"You *suppose* so! Don't you know it?"

"Well, now, she's a real nice little thing, Marilla. It's kind of a pity to send her back when she's so set on staying here."

"Matthew Cuthbert, you don't mean to say you think we ought to keep her!"

"Well, now, no, I suppose not—not exactly," stammered Matthew.

"I should say not. What good would she be to us?"

"We might be some good to her."

"Matthew Cuthbert! I can see as plain as day that you want to keep her."

"Well, now, she's a real interesting little thing," said Matthew. "You should have heard her talk coming from the station."

"Oh, she can talk fast enough. I saw that at once. But I don't like children who have so much to say. No, she's got to go back."

Matthew shrugged and went to bed. And after finishing the dishes, so did Marilla. And upstairs in the spare room, a lonely, friendless child cried herself to sleep.

[3]

Marilla Makes Up Her Mind

❖

IT WAS BROAD daylight when Anne awoke and sat up in bed, with sunshine pouring down through the window.

For a moment she could not remember where she was. Then it came to her. This was Green Gables! Oh, but they didn't want her because she wasn't a boy!

Still, it was morning, and there was a cherry tree in full bloom outside of her window. Anne dropped on her knees and gazed out into the June morning, her eyes shining with delight. Oh, wasn't it beautiful? Wasn't it a lovely place? If only she were staying here! She would imagine she was. There was scope for imagination here.

The huge cherry tree was so heavy with blossoms that hardly a leaf was to be seen. On both sides of the house was a big orchard, full of apple and cherry trees. The grass was all sprinkled with dandelions. And Anne could just see the brook running through some birch trees down in the hollow.

Anne was kneeling by the window, taking in the beauty of the place, when Marilla came into the bedroom.

"It's time you were dressed," Marilla said.

"Oh, isn't it wonderful?" said Anne, waving her hand at the outside world. "I can hear the brook laughing all the way up here. Have you ever noticed what cheerful things brooks are? They're always laughing. I'm so glad there's a brook near Green Gables. I shall always like to remember that there is a brook at Green Gables even if I never see it again. I'm not in the depths of despair this morning. I never can be in the morning. Isn't it a splendid thing that there are mornings? But I feel very sad. I've just been imagining that it was really me you wanted after all and that I was to stay here for ever and ever. It was a great comfort while it lasted."

"You'd better get dressed and come downstairs and never mind your imaginings," said Marilla as soon as she could get a word in edgewise. "Breakfast is waiting. Wash your face and comb your hair. Leave the window up and be as quick as you can."

When breakfast was finished, Anne offered to wash the dishes.

"Can you wash dishes right?" asked Marilla.

"Pretty well. I'm better at looking after children, though. I've had so much experience at that. It's such a pity you haven't any here for me to look after."

"I don't feel as if I wanted any more children to look after than I've got at present. *You're* problem enough! What's to be done with you, I don't know. Matthew is a most silly man."

"I think he's lovely," said Anne. "He didn't mind how much I talked—he seemed to like it. I felt that he was a kindred spirit as soon as ever I saw him."

"You're both odd enough, if that's what you mean by kindred spirits," said Marilla. "Yes, you may wash the dishes. Take plenty of hot water and be sure you dry them well. This afternoon we'll figure out what's to be done with you."

When Anne had finished with the dishes, Marilla told her she might go outside and amuse herself until lunchtime. Anne flew to the door, her eyes glowing. But then she stopped short, turned around, and came back and sat down by the table.

"What's the matter now?" demanded Marilla.

"I don't dare go out," said Anne. "If I can't stay here, there is no use in my loving Green Gables. And if I go out there and say hello to all those trees and flowers and the orchard and the brook, I won't be able to help loving it. It's hard enough now, so I won't make it any harder. I want to go out so much—everything seems to be calling to me, 'Anne, Anne, come out to us. Anne, Anne, we want a playmate'—but I'd better not. There is no use in loving things if you have to be torn from them, is there? And it's so hard to keep from loving things, isn't it? That was why I was so glad when I thought I was going to live here. I thought I'd have so many things to love. But that dream is over. I am resigned to my fate."

She is a *most* unusual child, thought Marilla, leaving Anne to herself at the table.

Later that day there was a knock at the door. Marilla found Mrs. Blewett at her doorstep and invited her in.

"This is certainly your lucky day," said the sour-looking lady as she took off her hat. "I heard in town that you've got an orphan girl you need to get rid of, and I'm here to take her off your hands. I need someone to help around the house. Now bring her over, I'm in a hurry."

Marilla did not look as if this were her lucky day. This was, indeed, her chance to get rid of the girl, but Marilla knew that Mrs. Blewett was a mean and stingy woman, and that if she gave Anne into her hands the poor child would be worked to death. Marilla shivered at the thought of Anne going with her.

Anne, meanwhile, had stepped forward from the hallway and was staring at Mrs. Blewett as if she were in a trance. Was she to be given to this mean-looking woman? She felt a lump coming up in her throat and was afraid she couldn't hold back her tears.

Mrs. Blewett darted her eyes over Anne from head to foot.

"How old are you and what's your name?" she demanded.

"Anne Shirley," said the child, "and I'm eleven years old."

"Humph! You're awful thin—but the thin ones sometimes make the best workers. I'll expect you to earn your keep, you know. Yes, I suppose I might as well take her off your hands, Miss Cuthbert."

Marilla looked at Anne and softened. "Well, I don't know. I didn't say that Matthew and I had absolutely decided that we wouldn't keep her. In fact, I believe we *are* likely to keep her. If we make up our minds not to keep her, we'll bring her over to you tomorrow night. If we don't, you may know that she is going to stay with us. Will that suit you, Mrs. Blewett?"

"I suppose it'll have to," said Mrs. Blewett.

During Marilla's speech a sunrise had dawned on Anne's face. And a moment later, when Mrs. Blewett had left, Anne flew across the room to Marilla.

"Oh, Miss Cuthbert, did you really say that perhaps you would let me stay at Green Gables?" she said in a whisper. "Did you really say it? Or did I only imagine that you did?"

"I think you'd better learn to control that imagination of yours, Anne, if you can't distinguish between what is real and what isn't," said Marilla. "Yes, you did hear me say just that. It isn't decided yet, and perhaps we will conclude to let Mrs. Blewett take you after all. She certainly needs you much more than I do."

"I'd rather go back to the orphanage than go live with her," said Anne. "She looks just like a—like a *ferret*."

Marilla agreed, but smothered her smile. "A little girl like you should be ashamed of talking like that," she said. "Go back and sit down quietly and hold your tongue and behave as a good girl should."

"I'll try to do and be anything you want me, if you'll only keep me," said Anne.

When Matthew came home that evening, Marilla told him the whole story. "Well, I guess we shall be keeping her," said Matthew, smiling widely.

"I've never brought up a child, especially a girl, and I dare say I'll make a terrible mess of it. But I'll do my best. So far as I'm concerned, Matthew, she may stay."

[4]

Anne's First Scrape

❖

MARILLA DECIDED NOT to tell Anne that she was to stay at Green Gables until the next afternoon. During the morning she kept the child busy with chores and watched over her while she did them. By noon she had concluded that Anne was smart and obedient, willing to work, and quick to learn. Her most serious shortcoming seemed to be a tendency to fall into daydreams in the middle of a task and forget all about it.

When Anne had finished washing the dinner dishes, she suddenly came up to Marilla and asked, "Oh, please, Miss Cuthbert, won't you tell me if you are going to send me away or not? I've tried to be patient all the morning, but I really cannot bear not knowing any longer. It's a dreadful feeling. Please tell me."

"Well," said Marilla, "I suppose I might as well tell you. Matthew and I have decided to keep you—that is, if you will try to be a good little girl and show yourself grateful. Why, child, whatever is the matter?"

"I'm crying," said Anne. "I can't think why. I'm glad as glad can be. Oh, I'm so happy! I'll try to be so good. It will be uphill work, I expect, for I've often been told I was desperately wicked. However, I'll do my very best. But can you tell me why I'm crying?"

"I suppose it's because you're all excited and worked up," said Marilla. "Sit down on that chair and try to calm yourself. Yes, you can stay here. You must go to school, of course, but it's vacation time until September."

"What am I to call you?" asked Anne. "Shall I always say Miss Cuthbert? Can I call you Aunt Marilla?"

"No. You'll just call me Marilla. I'm not used to being called Miss Cuthbert, and it would make me nervous."

"It sounds awfully disrespectful to say just Marilla," said Anne.

"I guess there'll be nothing disrespectful in it if you're careful to speak respectfully."

"But I'd love to call you Aunt Marilla," said Anne. "I've never had an aunt or any relation at all—not even a grandmother. It would make me feel as if I really belonged to you. Can't I call you Aunt Marilla?"

"No. I'm not your aunt, and I don't believe in calling people names that don't belong to them."

"But we could imagine you were my aunt."

"*I* couldn't," said Marilla.

"Don't you ever imagine things different from what they really are?" asked Anne.

"No."

"Oh!" Anne drew a long breath. "Oh, Miss—Marilla, how much you miss!"

Marilla rolled her eyes and sent Anne outside to play. What an unusual girl indeed!

Later that afternoon Marilla had a visitor to Green Gables. Mrs. Rachel Lynde, the town busybody, had come over to discover why Matthew and Marilla had not consulted her about the adoption of their orphan.

Anne was out in the orchard when Mrs. Lynde arrived, and she came running into the house when Marilla called. But when she saw a stranger in the parlor, she came to a dead halt.

"Well, they didn't pick you for your looks, that's sure and certain," was the first thing Mrs. Lynde said to Anne. "She's terrible skinny and homely, Marilla. Come here, child, and let me have a look at you. Did anyone ever see such freckles? And hair as red as carrots! Come here, child, I say."

With one bound Anne crossed the kitchen floor and stood before Mrs. Lynde, her face scarlet with anger and her whole body trembling from head to foot.

"I hate you!" she cried, stamping her foot on the floor. "I hate you—I hate you—I hate you! How dare you call me skinny and ugly? How dare you say I'm freckled and redheaded? You are a rude, impolite, unfeeling woman!"

"Anne!" cried Marilla.

"How dare you say such things about me?" Anne repeated. "How would you like to have such things said about you? How would you like to be told that you are fat and mean? I don't care if I do hurt your feelings by saying so! I hope I hurt them. You have hurt mine worse, and I'll *never* forgive you for it, never, never!"

"Anne, go to your room and stay there until I come up," said Marilla.

Anne, bursting into tears, rushed up to her room and slammed the door shut.

"Well, she certainly has a temper," said Mrs. Lynde.

Marilla turned to her and said, "You shouldn't have twitted her about her looks."

"Marilla Cuthbert, are you defending her?"

"No," said Marilla slowly, "I'm not trying to excuse her. She's been very naughty and will have to be taught a lesson. But you *were* too hard on her."

"Well—well!" said Mrs. Lynde, getting ready to leave. "I certainly did not expect to be insulted by *you*, Marilla. Good evening."

Marilla went upstairs and found Anne facedown on her bed and crying.

"Anne," she said softly.

No answer.

"Anne, get off that bed this minute and listen to what I have to say to you."

Anne squirmed off the bed and sat stiffly on a chair beside it, her eyes fixed stubbornly on the floor.

"Aren't you ashamed of yourself, Anne?"

"She hadn't any right to call me ugly and redheaded," was the answer.

"But you had no right to talk the way you did to her, Anne. I was ashamed of you," said Marilla.

"Just imagine how you would feel if somebody told you to your face that you were skinny and ugly," cried Anne.

"I'm not saying Mrs. Lynde was right in doing what she did," said Marilla. "But that is no excuse for such behavior on your part. She was a stranger and an elderly person and my guest—three very good reasons why you should have been respectful to her. You were rude and saucy and—and you must go to her and tell her you are very sorry for your bad temper and ask her to forgive you."

"I can never do that," said Anne. "You can punish me in any way you like, Marilla. You can shut me up in a dark, damp dungeon inhabited by snakes and toads and feed me only on bread and water and I shall not complain. But I cannot ask Mrs. Lynde to forgive me."

"We're not in the habit of shutting people up in dark, damp dungeons," said Marilla. "But you *will* apologize to Mrs. Lynde, and you'll stay here in your room until you tell me you're willing to do it."

"I shall have to stay here forever then," said Anne, "because I can't tell her I'm sorry. How can I? I'm *not* sorry. I'm *glad* I told her just what I did. I can't say I'm sorry when I'm not, can I? I can't even *imagine* I'm sorry."

"Then perhaps your imagination will be in better working order by the morning," said Marilla.

[5]

Anne's Apology

❖

THE NEXT DAY'S breakfast and lunch were very silent meals—for Anne remained stubborn and stayed in her room all day.

During the afternoon, when Marilla was out doing chores, Matthew went up to Anne's room and peeped in. Anne was sitting by the window gazing out into the garden. She looked very small and unhappy. Matthew softly closed the door and tiptoed over to her.

"Anne," he whispered. "How are you doing, Anne?"

"Pretty well. I imagine a good deal, and that helps to pass the time. Of course, it's rather lonesome. But then, I may as well get used to that."

Anne smiled, bravely facing the long years of imprisonment before her.

"Well, now, Anne, don't you think you'd better apologize and have it over with?" Matthew said. "It'll have to be done sooner or later, you know."

"I suppose I could do it for you," said Anne. "It would be true enough to say I am sorry, because I *am* sorry now. I wasn't a bit sorry last night. I was mad clear through, and I stayed mad all night. But this morning it was over, and I felt ashamed of myself. But I just *couldn't* think of going and telling Mrs. Lynde—it would be so humiliating. But still—I'd do anything for you—if you really want me to—"

"Well, now, of course I do. It's terrible lonesome downstairs without you. Just go and smooth things over. That's a good girl."

"Very well," said Anne. "I'll tell Marilla as soon as she comes in."

"That's right—that's right, Anne. Good girl."

That afternoon Anne went with Marilla to Mrs. Lynde's house. When they arrived, Anne went up to Mrs. Lynde and, before saying a thing, she went down on her knees and held out her hands.

"Oh, Mrs. Lynde, I am so extremely sorry," she said. "I could never express all my sorrow, no, not if I used up a whole dictionary. You must just imagine it. I behaved terribly to you—and I've disgraced my dear friends,

Matthew and Marilla, who have let me stay at Green Gables although I'm not a boy. I'm a dreadfully wicked and ungrateful girl, and I deserve to be punished forever. It was very wicked of me to fly into a temper because you told me the truth. It *was* the truth—every word you said was true. My hair is red, and I'm freckled and skinny and ugly. What I said to you was true, too, but I shouldn't have said it. Oh, Mrs. Lynde, please, please forgive me. If you refuse, it will be a lifelong sorrow to me. Please say you forgive me, Mrs. Lynde."

Anne bowed her head and waited for the word of judgment.

Marilla felt Anne's apology was overly dramatic, but Anne was clearly sincere, and Mrs. Lynde seemed more than satisfied.

"There, there, get up, child," Mrs. Lynde said. "Of course I forgive you. I guess I was a little too hard on you. It can't be denied your hair is terribly red. But I knew a girl once whose hair was every bit as red as yours when she was young, but when she grew up it darkened to a real handsome auburn. I wouldn't be at all surprised if yours did, too."

"Oh, Mrs. Lynde!" Anne said as she rose to her feet. "You have given me a hope! I shall always consider you my great friend!"

"Now run along, child. And you can pick a bouquet of white lilies over in the corner if you like." And Anne ran out into the sunshine, happy as a prisoner freed from her cell.

Anne Finds a Friend

❖

"WELL, HOW DO you like them?" asked Marilla.

Anne was standing in her room, looking at three new dresses spread out on the bed. Marilla had made them up herself, and they were all made alike—plain skirts with plain waists, and sleeves as plain and tight as sleeves could be.

"I'll imagine that I like them," said Anne softly.

"I don't want you to *imagine* it," said Marilla. "Oh, I can see you don't like the dresses! What is the matter with them? Aren't they neat and clean and new?"

"Yes."

"Then why don't you like them?"

"They're—they're not—pretty," said Anne.

"Pretty!" Marilla said. "Those are good, sensible dresses,

without any frills about them, and they're all you'll get this summer. I should think you'd be grateful."

"Oh, I *am* grateful," said Anne. "But I'd be ever so much gratefuller if—if you'd made just one of them with puffed sleeves. Puffed sleeves are so fashionable now. It would give me such a thrill, Marilla, just to wear a dress with puffed sleeves."

"Well, you'll have to do without your thrill. I hadn't any material to waste on puffed sleeves. I prefer the plain, sensible ones. Now hang those dresses carefully up in your closet."

Anne clasped her hands and looked at the dresses. "I was hoping for puffed sleeves," she murmured to herself, but Marilla didn't hear.

"I've got some news for you," Marilla said, hoping to cheer the girl up. "Diana Barry came home this afternoon. I'm going up to see if I can borrow a skirt pattern from Mrs. Barry, and if you like, you can come with me and get acquainted with Diana. She's nearly your age, you know."

Anne rose to her feet. "Oh, Marilla, I'm frightened. What if she doesn't like me! It would be the most tragical disappointment of my life."

"Now, don't get into a fluster. And I do wish you wouldn't use such long words. It sounds so funny in a little girl. I guess Diana'll like you well enough."

"Oh, Marilla, you'd be excited, too, if you were going to meet a little girl you hoped to be your bosom friend," she said.

They went over to the Barrys' house by the shortcut across the brook. Mrs. Barry came to the kitchen door in answer to Marilla's knock.

"How do you do, Marilla?" she said. "Come in. And is this the little girl you've adopted?"

"Yes, this is Anne Shirley," said Marilla.

"Spelled with an *e*," added Anne.

"Yes, well, how are you, dear?"

"I am well in body, although considerable rumpled up in spirit, thank you, ma'am," said Anne. Marilla smiled to herself at this.

Diana was sitting on the sofa, reading a book, which she dropped when the visitors came in.

"This is my little girl Diana," said Mrs. Barry. "Diana, why don't you take Anne out into the garden and show her your flowers?"

"Oh, Diana," said Anne once they were outside, "do you think—oh, do you think you can like me a little—enough to be my bosom friend?"

Diana laughed.

"Why, I guess so," she said. "I'm awfully glad you've

come to live at Green Gables. It will be jolly to have somebody to play with."

"Will you swear to be my friend for ever and ever?" asked Anne.

Diana wrinkled her brow in thought. After a long moment, she said, "Yes. *Let's* be friends forever."

When Marilla and Anne went home, Diana went with them as far as the log bridge. The two little girls walked with their arms about each other. At the brook they promised to meet the next morning to go to the first day of school together.

"Well," said Marilla once they were home, "did you find Diana a kindred spirit?"

"Oh, yes," sighed Anne. "Marilla, I'm the happiest girl on Prince Edward Island this very moment, I assure you."

The next morning Anne and her bosom friend walked to the schoolhouse. It was a low building with wide windows and sat beside a brook where the children could keep their bottles of milk cold and sweet until lunchtime.

Anne's experience at school started off well enough. She was very bright and looked as if she might be the top scholar in her class. Diana, however, told her that she might have some competition from Gilbert Blythe.

"Gilbert Blythe?" asked Anne.

"That's him sitting across the aisle from you. Just look at him and see if you don't think he's handsome."

Anne looked over at Gilbert Blythe, only to see that he was already looking at *her*. He smiled and winked at Anne.

"I think your Gilbert Blythe *is* handsome," said Anne to Diana, "but I think he's very bold. It isn't good manners to wink at a strange girl."

But it was not until the afternoon that things really began to happen.

The teacher was back in the corner explaining a problem in algebra to Prissy Andrews, and the other students were doing pretty much as they pleased—eating green apples, whispering, drawing pictures on their slates. Gilbert Blythe was trying to make Anne Shirley look at him and failing, because Anne was staring out the window and daydreaming.

Gilbert Blythe wasn't used to trying to make a girl look at him and failing. So he reached across the aisle, picked up the end of Anne's long red braid, held it out at arm's length, and whispered, "Carrots! Carrots!"

Anne sprang up and glared at him. "You mean, hateful boy!" she cried. "How dare you!"

And then—*thwack!* Anne brought her slate down on

Gilbert's head and cracked it—the slate, not his head.

All the students said "Oh!" at once, and the teacher came down the aisle and laid his hand on Anne's shoulder.

"Anne Shirley, what's the meaning of this?" he said angrily.

Anne would not answer. She *could* not tell the whole school that she had been called "carrots."

But just then Gilbert said, "It was my fault, sir. I teased her."

The teacher ignored him and turned back to Anne. "Go and stand on the platform in front of the blackboard for the rest of the afternoon."

Anne did as she was told and stood there the rest of the afternoon. She did not cry or hang her head. Her anger was still too hot. As for Gilbert Blythe, she would not even look at him. She would *never* look at him again! She would never speak to him!!

When school was dismissed, Gilbert went over to speak with Anne. "I'm awfully sorry I made fun of your hair, Anne. Honest I am. Don't be mad for keeps, now."

Anne swept by without even looking at him.

But Gilbert was ready for this, so he caught up to her and slipped a little pink candy heart into her hand. It had a little gold saying on it: "You are sweet."

Anne took the pink heart gingerly between the tips of her fingers, dropped it on the floor, ground it to powder beneath her heel, and walked away. "I'll never, *ever* forgive Gilbert Blythe," she repeated to herself all the way home to Green Gables.

[7]

A Tragical Tea

❖

MARILLA COULD TELL that Anne was feeling out of sorts that week, so she suggested something to make her feel a little better. "Anne, you can ask Diana to come over and spend the afternoon with you and have tea while I'm in town."

"Oh, Marilla!" Anne clasped her hands. "How perfectly lovely! How did you know I've longed for that very thing? It will seem so nice and grown-uppish. Oh, Marilla, can I use the fancy tea set?"

"No, indeed! You'll use the old brown tea set. But you can open the little yellow crock of cherry preserves. And you can cut some fruitcake and have some of the cookies."

"I can just imagine myself sitting down at the head of

the table and pouring out the tea," said Anne, "and asking Diana if she takes sugar! I know she doesn't, but of course I'll ask her just as if I didn't know. Oh, Marilla, it's wonderful just to think of it. Can I take her into the parlor to sit?"

"No. The sitting room will do for you and your company. But there's a half-bottle of raspberry cordial that you and Diana can have if you like."

Anne flew to Diana's house to invite her, and half an hour later Diana arrived at Green Gables, all dressed up. At other times Diana would run into the kitchen without knocking, but now she knocked properly at the front door. And when Anne opened it, both little girls shook hands.

"And how is your mother?" asked Anne politely, as if she hadn't just seen Mrs. Barry.

"She is very well, thank you. I hope Mr. Cuthbert is well, and Miss Cuthbert?" said Diana.

"Very well, thank you. Would you like some tea, Diana? Or perhaps some lovely raspberry cordial to start?"

"Oh, yes, please. I'd love some of the cordial."

Anne looked on the second shelf of the pantry, but there was no bottle of raspberry cordial there. Soon, however, she saw it way back on the top shelf. She put it on a tray and set it on the table with a glass.

"Now, please help yourself, Diana," Anne said politely. "I don't believe I'll have any just now."

Diana poured herself out a glassful, looked at its bright red color, and then sipped it daintily.

"That's awfully nice raspberry cordial, Anne," she said. "I didn't know raspberry cordial was so nice."

"I'm real glad you like it. Take as much as you want. I'm going to run out and stir the fire up. There are so many responsibilities when one keeps house, aren't there?"

When Anne came back from the kitchen, Diana was drinking her second glassful of cordial, and when Anne offered, she drank a third. The raspberry cordial was certainly very nice.

But soon Diana began to look pale.

"Why, Diana, what is the matter?"

Diana had stood up very unsteadily. Then she sat down again, putting her hands to her head.

"I'm—I'm awful sick," she said. "I—I—must go right home."

"Oh, you mustn't dream of going home without your tea," cried Anne. "I'll get it right away."

"I must go home," repeated Diana.

"Let me get you a lunch anyhow," pleaded Anne. "Let me give you a bit of fruitcake and some of the cherry preserves. Lie down on the sofa for a little while, and you'll be better. Where do you feel bad?"

"I must go home," said Diana, and that was all she would say.

"I never heard of company going home without tea," Anne cried. "Oh, Diana, do you suppose you have the smallpox? If you do, I'll go and nurse you, you can depend on that. I'll never forsake you. But I do wish you'd stay till after tea. Where do you feel bad?"

"I'm awful dizzy," said Diana.

And indeed, she walked home very dizzily.

The next day Marilla sent Anne to the Barrys' on an errand. In a very short time Anne came flying back up the lane with tears rolling down her cheeks.

"Whatever is wrong now, Anne?" asked Marilla.

"Mrs. Barry says that I got Diana *drunk* yesterday, and she says I must be a thoroughly bad, wicked little girl, and she's never, never going to let Diana play with me again. Oh, Marilla, I'm just overcome with woe."

"Got Diana drunk!" Marilla cried. "Anne, are you crazy or is Mrs. Barry? What on earth did you give Diana?"

"Not a thing but raspberry cordial," sobbed Anne. "I never thought raspberry cordial would get people drunk, Marilla—not even if they drank three big glassfuls, as Diana did. Oh, I didn't mean to get her drunk."

"Drunk, fiddlesticks!" said Marilla, going into the sitting room pantry. There on the shelf was a bottle which she at once recognized. It was her homemade wine, and *not* the raspberry cordial. She now remembered that she had put the cordial down in the cellar instead of in the pantry, as she had told Anne.

She went back to the kitchen with the wine bottle in her hand.

"Anne, you certainly have a genius for getting into trouble. You went and gave Diana wine instead of raspberry cordial. Didn't you know the difference yourself?"

"I never tasted it," said Anne. "I thought it was the cordial. Diana got awfully sick and had to go home. Mrs. Barry says Diana laughed silly-like when she asked her what was the matter, and she went to sleep and slept for hours. She smelled her breath and knew she was drunk. She thinks I did it on purpose."

"There, there, child, don't cry. I can see you weren't to blame," said Marilla.

"I *must* cry," said Anne. "My heart is broken. Diana and I are parted forever. Oh, Marilla, I little dreamed of this when first we swore our vows of friendship."

"Don't be foolish, Anne. Mrs. Barry will think better of it when she finds you're not to blame. I'll go speak with her, and everything will be all right."

But when she came back from the Barrys', Marilla was sad to report that everything would not be all right. "Mrs. Barry refuses to believe you, Anne. I'm sorry."

"Oh, I am truly in the depths of despair now, Marilla," cried Anne.

[8]

Anne to the Rescue

❖

THE NEXT AFTERNOON Anne, bending over her knitting at the kitchen window, happened to look out and see Diana waving in the yard. Anne flew out of the house, thinking they could be friends again, but her hope faded when she saw Diana's sad face.

"Your mother hasn't relented?" Anne asked.

Diana shook her head.

"No. And oh, Anne, she says I'm never to play with you again. I've cried and cried and told her it wasn't your fault, but it wasn't any use. She said I could say good-bye to you, but I was only to stay ten minutes."

"Ten minutes isn't very long to say an eternal farewell in," said Anne. "Oh, Diana, will you promise faithfully never to forget me?"

"Indeed, I will," cried Diana, "and I'll never have another bosom friend—I don't even want to. I couldn't love anybody as I love you."

"Oh, Diana," cried Anne, "do you *love* me?"

"Why, of course I do. Didn't you know that?"

"No, I never hoped you *loved* me. Why, Diana, I didn't think anybody could love me. Nobody ever has loved me since I can remember. Oh, this is wonderful! It's a ray of light that will forever shine on the darkness of a path apart from thee, Diana. Oh, just say it once again."

"I love you, Anne," said Diana, "and I always will, you may be sure of that."

"And I will always love thee, Diana," said Anne. "Fare thee well, my beloved friend. Henceforth we must be as strangers, but my heart will ever be faithful to thee."

Anne stood and watched Diana out of sight before going back inside.

"It is all over," she told Marilla. "I shall never have another friend. Diana and I said farewell down by the spring. It will be sacred in my memory forever. I used the most pathetic language I could think of and said 'thou' and 'thee.' 'Thou' and 'thee' seem so much more romantic than 'you.' Alas, I don't believe I'll live very long. Perhaps when she sees me lying cold and dead Mrs. Barry may feel sorry for what she has done."

"I don't think there is much fear of your dying of grief as long as you can talk, Anne," said Marilla, smiling.

For several weeks Diana heeded her mother and didn't try to speak with her friend. So Anne was very surprised when Diana burst into Green Gables one night as Matthew and Anne were sitting down to dinner alone. Marilla was visiting a friend.

"What's the matter, Diana?" cried Anne. "Has your mother relented at last?"

"Oh, Anne, do come quick," cried Diana. "My sister is awful sick—she's got croup. Father and Mother are away to town, and there's nobody to go for the doctor. Minnie May is awful bad, and I don't know what to do— and oh, Anne, I'm so scared!"

Matthew, without a word, reached out for his cap and coat and went away into the darkness of the yard.

"He's gone for the doctor," said Anne, who was putting on her jacket. "I know it as well as if he'd said so. Matthew and I are such kindred spirits I can read his thoughts without words at all."

"What if he doesn't find the doctor?" sobbed Diana.

"It's all right, Diana. I know exactly what to do for croup. Just wait till I get the ipecac bottle—you might not have any at your house. Come on now."

The two little girls hurried to the Barrys'.

45

Minnie May, aged three, was really very sick. She lay on the kitchen sofa, and her breathing could be heard all over the house. Anne went to work with skill and promptness.

"Minnie May has croup, all right. She's pretty bad, but I've seen them worse. First we must have lots of hot water. I declare, Diana, there isn't more than a cupful in the kettle! There, I've filled it up. Now put some wood in the stove. I'll undress Minnie May and put her to bed, but I'm going to give her a dose of ipecac first."

Minnie May did not like the medicine, but Anne made sure she took all her doses through the long night.

It was three o'clock when Matthew finally came with a doctor, but by then Minnie May was much better and sleeping soundly.

"I was awfully near giving up in despair," Anne told the doctor. "She got worse and worse, and I actually thought she was going to choke to death. I gave her every drop of ipecac in that bottle, and then finally she coughed up the phlegm and began to get better right away. You can just imagine my relief, Doctor."

"Yes, I know," nodded the doctor. Later on he told Mr. and Mrs. Barry that "that little redheaded girl is as smart as they make 'em. I tell you, she saved that baby's life, for it would have been too late by the time I got here."

The next day Marilla had something to tell Anne. "Mrs. Barry was here this afternoon," she said. "She wanted to see you, but I wouldn't wake you up. She says you saved Minnie May's life, and she is very sorry she acted as she did about that wine. She says she knows now you didn't mean to get Diana drunk, and she hopes you'll forgive her and be good friends with Diana again. You're to go over this afternoon if you like. Now, Anne Shirley, for pity's sake, don't fly clean up into the air."

But the warning was useless, for Anne was out of the house running toward Diana's even before Marilla had finished her sentence.

[9]

Another Scrape

❖

THE SCHOOL YEAR ended with Diana and Anne happy, bosom friends again. And that summer rolled by in what seemed to Anne like no time at all.

When fall arrived, Anne's class had a new teacher, Miss Allan, with whom Anne promptly fell in love. Miss Allan was another kindred spirit.

"She's perfectly lovely," Anne explained to Marilla one afternoon. "She's taken our class, and she's a splendid teacher. She said right away she didn't think it was fair for the teacher to ask all the questions, and you know, Marilla, that is exactly what I've always thought. She said we could ask her any question we liked, and I asked ever so many. I'm good at asking questions, Marilla."

"I believe you," said Marilla. "Do you suppose we should have her to tea someday soon?"

Anne nearly jumped out of her seat. "Oh, Marilla, *can* we? Will you let me make a cake for the occasion? I'd love to do something for Miss Allan, and you know, I can make a pretty good cake by this time."

"You may make a layer cake," promised Marilla.

All week Anne helped Marilla prepare Green Gables for Miss Allan's visit. Anne was wild with excitement and delight. She talked it all over with Diana Tuesday night in the twilight.

"Oh, Diana, what if my layer cake isn't any good?"

"It'll be good, all right," answered Diana.

"But cakes have such a terrible habit of turning out bad just when you especially want them to be good," sighed Anne.

Saturday morning came. Anne got up at sunrise because she was too excited to sleep. After breakfast she proceeded to make her cake. When she finally shut the oven door upon it she drew a long breath.

"I'm sure I haven't forgotten anything this time, Marilla. But do you think it will rise? Marilla, what if the cake doesn't rise?"

"We'll have plenty without it," said Marilla.

The cake did rise, however, and came out of the oven

as light and feathery as golden foam. Anne clapped it together with layers of ruby jelly. Perhaps, she thought, Miss Allan would like it enough to ask for a second piece!

Miss Allan arrived, and she chatted with Matthew and Marilla and Anne over tea. All was going merry as a marriage bell until Anne's layer cake was passed. Miss Allan, who had already been served a great deal of food, declined it. But Marilla, seeing the disappointment on Anne's face, said smilingly:

"Oh, you must take a piece of this, Miss Allan. Anne made it on purpose for you."

"In that case, I must sample it," laughed Miss Allan, helping herself to a nice big piece.

Miss Allan took a mouthful, and a most peculiar expression crossed her face. She didn't say a word, however, but ate away at it. Marilla saw her face and hurried to taste the cake.

"Anne Shirley!" she exclaimed. "What on earth did you put into that cake?"

"Nothing but what the recipe said, Marilla," cried Anne. "Oh, isn't it all right?"

"All right! It's simply horrible. Miss Allan, don't try to eat it. Anne, taste it yourself. What flavoring did you use?"

"Vanilla," said Anne, her face red with embarrassment. "Only vanilla. Oh, Marilla! What happened?"

"Go and bring me the bottle of vanilla you used."

Anne went to the pantry and returned with a small bottle filled with a brown liquid and labeled "Vanilla."

Marilla took it, uncorked it, smelled it.

"Mercy, Anne, you've flavored that cake with *liniment*. I broke the liniment bottle last week and poured what was left into an old empty vanilla bottle. I suppose it's partly my fault—I should have warned you—but couldn't you have smelled it?"

Tears began streaming down Anne's face.

"I couldn't—I had such a cold!" and with this she ran up to her room and threw herself on her bed.

Soon she heard a step on the stairs, and somebody entered the room.

"Oh, Marilla," cried Anne, without looking up, "I'm disgraced forever. I shall never be able to live this down. Diana will ask me how my cake turned out, and I shall have to tell her the truth. I shall always be pointed at as the girl who flavored a cake with liniment. Gil—the boys in school will never get over laughing at it. Oh, I cannot ever look Miss Allan in the face again. Perhaps she'll think I tried to poison her. But the liniment isn't poisonous. It's meant to be taken internally—

although not in cakes. Won't you tell Miss Allan so, Marilla?"

"Suppose you tell her so yourself," said a merry voice.

Anne flew up, to find Miss Allan standing by her bed, looking at her with laughing eyes.

"My dear little girl, you mustn't cry like this," she said. "Why, it's all just a funny mistake that anybody might make."

"Oh, no, it takes *me* to make such a mistake," said Anne. "And I wanted to have that cake so nice for you, Miss Allan."

"Yes, I know, dear. And I assure you I appreciate your kindness just as much as if it had turned out all right. Now, you mustn't cry anymore, but come down with me and show me your flower garden."

Nothing more was said about the liniment cake, but when Miss Allan was gone, Marilla laughingly said, "I never saw a girl who could make mistakes like you, Anne."

"Yes, I know it," admitted Anne. "But have you ever noticed one thing about me, Marilla? I never make the same mistake twice."

"I don't know as that's much benefit when you're always making new ones."

"Oh, don't you see, Marilla? There must be a limit to

the mistakes one person can make, and when I get to the end of them, then I'll be through with them. That's a very comforting thought."

Marilla just smiled and went out to feed the liniment cake to the pigs.

10

Anne Dyes Her Hair

❖

MARILLA WALKED BACK from town one late April evening, looking forward to a snapping wood fire and a table nicely spread for dinner.

But when Marilla entered her kitchen and found the fire out, with no sign of Anne anywhere, she felt disappointed and a bit angry. She had told Anne to be sure and have dinner ready at five o'clock, but now she must hurry to prepare the meal herself.

"I'll have a little chat with Anne when she comes home," said Marilla as she prepared the meal. Matthew had come in and was waiting for his dinner in the corner. "She's off somewhere with Diana, I'm sure, and never thinking once about the time or her duties. I don't care if Miss Allan does say she's the brightest and sweetest child in her class. She may be bright and sweet, but she's full of nonsense, too, and who knows what scrape she'll get into next."

It was dark when supper was ready, but still no sign of Anne. Matthew and Marilla ate and then washed and put away the dishes, but still the girl had not come home. Then, needing a candle, Marilla went up to Anne's room for the one that stood on Anne's table. Lighting it, she turned around to see Anne herself lying on the bed, facedown among the pillows.

"Mercy!" cried Marilla. "Have you been asleep, Anne?"

"No," was the muffled reply.

"Are you sick then?"

Anne buried herself deeper into her pillows.

"No. But please, Marilla, go away and don't look at me. I'm in the depths of despair and I don't care who gets the best-student award in class. Little things like that are of no importance now, because I'll never be able to go anywhere again. Please, Marilla, go away and don't look at me."

"Anne Shirley, whatever is the matter with you? What have you done? Get right up this minute and tell me. This minute, I say. There now, what is it?"

Anne slid to the floor.

"Look at my hair, Marilla," she whispered.

Marilla lifted her candle and looked at Anne's hair, flowing down her back.

"Anne Shirley, what have you done to your hair? Why, it's *green*!"

Green it was—an ugly dull green, with only streaks here and there of the original red.

"Yes, it's green," moaned Anne. "I thought nothing could be as bad as red hair. But now I know it's ten times worse to have green hair. Oh, Marilla, I am utterly wretched."

"Come right down to the kitchen and tell me what you've done. I've been expecting something like this for some time. You haven't got into any scrape for over two months, and I was sure another one was due. Now, then, what did you do to your hair?"

"I dyed it."

"Dyed it! Dyed your hair! Anne Shirley, didn't you know it was a wicked thing to do?"

"Yes, I knew it was a little wicked," admitted Anne. "But I thought it was worthwhile to be a little wicked to get rid of red hair. I meant to be extra good in other ways to make up for it."

"Well," said Marilla, "if I had done it, I'd at least have dyed it a decent color. I wouldn't have dyed my hair green."

"But I didn't mean to dye it green, Marilla," said Anne. "He said it would turn my hair a beautiful raven black. How could I doubt his word, Marilla?"

"Who said? Who are you talking about?"

"The peddler that was here this afternoon. I bought the dye from him. He said it would dye any hair a beautiful raven black and wouldn't wash off. The temptation was irresistible. So I bought it, and as soon as he had gone I came up here and applied it with an old hairbrush, as the directions said. I used up the whole bottle, and oh, Marilla, my hair turned green!"

"Well, I hope you see where your vanity has led you, Anne. I suppose the first thing is to give your hair a good washing and see if that will do any good."

So Anne washed her hair, scrubbing it with soap and water, but it made no difference.

"Oh, Marilla, what shall I do?" asked Anne in tears. "I can never live this down. People have pretty well forgotten my other mistakes—the liniment cake and getting Diana drunk and flying into a temper with Mrs. Lynde. But they'll never forget this. Oh, Marilla, I am the unhappiest girl on Prince Edward Island."

Anne's unhappiness continued for a week. During that time she went nowhere and shampooed her hair every day. Only Diana knew her secret, but she promised never to tell, and she kept her word. At the end of the week Marilla said, "It's no use, Anne. Your hair must be cut off, there is no other way. You can't go out with it looking like that."

Anne's lips quivered, but she went for the scissors herself.

"Please cut it off at once, Marilla, and have it over. Oh, I feel that my heart is broken. This is such an unromantic affliction. I'm going to weep all the time you're cutting it off, if it won't interfere. It seems such a tragical thing."

Marilla did her work thoroughly, cutting Anne's hair as closely as possible. The result was not becoming, to state the case mildly. Anne turned her mirror to the wall.

"I'll never, never look at myself again until my hair grows," she cried.

Then she suddenly righted the mirror.

"Yes, I will, too. It will be my punishment. I'll look at myself every time I come to my room and see how ugly I am. And I won't try to imagine it away either. I never thought I was vain about my hair, of all things, but now I know I was, in spite of its being red, because it was so long and thick and curly."

11

Gilbert to the Rescue

❋

IT WAS A month or so later when Anne was walking by the pond, in the flickering shadow of the birch trees. Her hair had begun to grow back nicely. It was full and curly and—to Anne's great happiness—it was growing back a shade closer to auburn.

Anne was absorbed in a particularly romantic daydream, so she did not hear the approach of her archrival, Gilbert Blythe. As Gilbert watched, he saw Anne walk onto the little bridge over the stream that fed the pond, bend down, and reach out for a flower. But just as she grasped its wispy fronds—*plunk*—she fell straight into the water.

In a flash Gilbert ran over and jumped in to save Anne, though he soon found that the water was only knee-deep. Anne, who was still a bit shocked to find herself in the water, was doubly confused to find herself being held by Gilbert Blythe.

"I'm—I'm very much obliged," she said. They were the first words she had spoken to Gilbert in two years. Then she turned away and hurried up the bank.

But Gilbert laid a hand on her arm. "Anne," he said, "look here. Can't we be good friends? I'm awfully sorry I made fun of your hair that time. I didn't mean to vex you, and I only meant it for a joke. Besides, it's so long ago. I think your hair is awfully pretty now—honest I do. Let's be friends."

For a moment Anne hesitated. She had an odd feeling that the half-shy, half-eager expression in Gilbert's hazel eyes was something that was very good to see. Her heart gave a quick little beat. But then the scene of two years before flashed back to her memory, as if it had taken place yesterday. Gilbert had called her "carrots" and had brought about her disgrace before the whole school. She would never forgive him!

"No," she said coldly, "I shall never be friends with you, Gilbert Blythe. And I don't want to be!"

"All right!" Gilbert walked off with an angry color in his cheeks. "I'll never ask you to be friends again, Anne Shirley. And I don't care either!"

Anne held her head very high, but she had an odd feeling of regret. She almost wished she had answered Gilbert differently. Of course he had insulted her terribly, but still—!

When Anne told Diana the story later, Diana remarked, "Oh, Anne, how splendid of him! Why, it's so romantic! Of course you'll speak to him after this."

"Of course I won't," said Anne. "And I don't want ever to hear the word *romantic* again, Diana."

By that evening Matthew and Marilla had heard about Anne falling into the stream.

"Will you ever have any sense, Anne?" asked Marilla.

"Oh, yes, I think I will, Marilla," answered Anne. "I think my prospects of becoming sensible are brighter now than ever."

"I don't see how," said Marilla.

"Well," explained Anne, "I've learned a new and valuable lesson today. I have come to the conclusion that it is no use trying to be romantic on Prince Edward Island. It was probably easy enough in Camelot hundreds of years ago, but romance is too unlikely now. I feel quite sure that you will soon see a great improvement in me in this respect, Marilla."

"I certainly hope so," said Marilla.

But Matthew, who had been sitting quietly in his

corner, laid a hand on Anne's shoulder when Marilla had gone out.

"Don't give up all your romance, Anne," he whispered shyly. "A little of it is a good thing—not too much of course—but keep a little of it, Anne, keep a little of it."

12

Anne Changes Her Mind

❖

AFTER THAT DAY by the pond, Gilbert Blythe ignored Anne Shirley. He talked with the other girls, exchanged books and puzzles with them, discussed lessons and plans, and sometimes walked them home. But Anne Shirley he simply ignored, and Anne found out that it is not pleasant to be ignored. She told herself with a toss of her head that she did not care. But deep down she knew that she did care, and that if she had that chance at the pond again she would answer very differently. Anne now realized that she had forgiven Gilbert without knowing it. But it was too late.

However, for the most part, Anne was happy, for there were lessons to be learned and honors to be won and delightful books to read. The winter passed away in a round of pleasant duties and studies. And then, almost before Anne realized it, another spring and summer had come and gone.

As the seasons went by, Anne grew—shooting up so rapidly that Marilla was astonished one day, when they were standing side by side, to find the girl was taller than herself.

"Why, Anne, how you've grown!" she said. The child she had learned to love had vanished somehow, and here was this tall, serious-eyed girl of fifteen.

There were other changes in Anne, too. For one thing, she became much quieter. Perhaps she thought and dreamed as much as ever, but she certainly talked less. Marilla noticed and commented on this one day.

"You don't chatter half as much as you used to, Anne, nor use half as many big words. What has come over you?"

Anne laughed a little as she dropped her book and looked dreamily out of the window. "I don't know—I don't want to talk as much," she said. "It's fun to be almost grown up in some ways, but it's not the kind of fun I expected, Marilla. There's so much to learn and do and think that there isn't time for big words."

"Anne, I have some news for you that I think you'll like," Marilla said.

"Yes, Marilla, what is it?"

"Well, Miss Allan wants to organize a class among her advanced students who want to study for the entrance examination into Queen's College. She intends to give them extra lessons for an hour after school. And she came to ask Matthew and me if we would like to have you join it. What do you think about it yourself, Anne? Would you like to go to Queen's and study to be a teacher?"

"Oh, Marilla!" cried Anne. "It's been the dream of my life. But I didn't say anything about it because I supposed it would be perfectly useless. I'd love to be a teacher. But won't it be dreadfully expensive?"

"I guess you needn't worry about that part of it. When Matthew and I took you to bring up, we decided you would get a good education. We've been saving ever since! I believe in a girl being fitted to earn her own living whether she ever has to or not. So you can join the Queen's class if you like, Anne."

"Oh, Marilla, thank you. I'll study as hard as I can and do my very best to be a credit to you. I warn you not to expect much in geometry, but I think I can hold my own in anything else if I work hard."

"I dare say you'll get along well enough. Miss Allan says you are quite bright." Marilla didn't want to tell

Anne that Miss Allan had said that Anne was one of the brightest students she'd ever had.

The Queen's class was organized and included Anne, Ruby Gillis, Josie Pye, and Gilbert Blythe. There was now open rivalry between Gilbert and Anne. The two were competing for top honors in the school, and the other members of the class never dreamed of trying to compete with them. But Gilbert and Anne would still not talk with each other.

"You've only two more months before the entrance examination," said Marilla one day. "Do you think you'll be able to get through?"

Anne shivered.

"I don't know. Sometimes I think I'll be all right— and then I get horribly afraid. Sometimes I wake up in the night and wonder what I'll do if I don't pass."

"Why, go to school next year and try again," said Marilla.

"Oh, I don't believe I'd have the heart for it. It would be such a disgrace to fail, especially if Gil—if the others passed."

The time for the examination soon came, and Anne went to town to sit for it. When she returned, Diana demanded a full report. "Oh, Anne. How did you do on your test?"

"Pretty well, I think, in everything but the geometry. I don't know whether I passed in it or not, and I have a creepy feeling that I didn't."

"How did the others do?"

"The girls say they know they didn't pass, but I think they did pretty well. But we don't really know anything about it and won't until the pass list is out. That won't be for a fortnight. I wish I could go to sleep and never wake up until it is over."

Diana knew it would be useless to ask how Gilbert Blythe had done, so she merely said, "Oh, you'll pass all right. Don't worry."

"I'd rather not pass at all than do worse than Gil—" started Anne, but then stopped. Anne was wishing more and more that she had made friends with Gilbert when he asked her, but now she hoped to do better than him in the examination.

But she also wished to "pass high" for the sake of Matthew and Marilla—especially Matthew. Matthew had told her that she "would beat the whole island." That, Anne felt, was something it would be foolish to hope for even in her wildest dreams. But she did hope to be among the first ten at least, so that she might see Matthew's kindly brown eyes gleam with pride.

One evening the news came. Anne was sitting at her

open window when she saw Diana come flying over the log bridge and up the slope, with a newspaper in her hand.

Anne sprang to her feet, knowing at once what that paper contained. The pass list was out! Her head whirled and her heart beat until it hurt her.

"Anne, you've passed," Diana cried, "passed the *very first*—you and Gilbert both—you're tied—but your name is first. Oh, I'm so proud!"

Anne quivered with excitement. "Excuse me a minute, Diana. I must run right out to the field to tell Matthew and Marilla."

They hurried to the hayfield below the barn where Matthew was coiling hay with Marilla.

"Oh, Matthew! Marilla!" cried Anne. "I've passed and I'm first—or one of the first!"

"Well, now, I always said it," said Matthew. "I knew you could beat them all easy."

"You've done pretty well, I must say, Anne," said Marilla, trying to hide her extreme pride in Anne, but failing utterly. To herself, she had already promised Anne a new dress with the puffiest sleeves on Prince Edward Island.

That evening Anne sat by the fire talking with Matthew. "I'll be going off to university next year, dear Matthew, and you'll have even less help around here. Oh, sometimes I wish I *had* been the boy you sent for. I'd have been able to help you so much more and spare you in a hundred ways. I could find it in my heart to wish I had been, just for that."

"Well, now, I'd rather have you than a dozen boys, Anne," said Matthew, patting her hand. "Just mind you that—rather than a dozen boys. Well, now, I guess it wasn't a boy that passed first in Prince Edward Island, was it? It was a girl—my girl—my girl that I'm proud of."

He smiled his shy smile at her and went out into the yard. Anne took the memory of it with her when she went to her room that night and sat for a long while at her open window, thinking of the past and dreaming of the future.

The next day Anne helped Marilla with the chores in the kitchen. "Gilbert Blythe is going to Queen's, too, isn't he?" Marilla asked.

"Yes," said Anne.

"What a nice-looking fellow he is," said Marilla. "I saw him in town last Sunday, and he seemed so tall and manly. He looks a lot like his father did at the same age. John Blythe was a nice boy. We used to be real good friends, he and I. People called him my boyfriend."

Anne looked up with swift interest.

"Oh, Marilla—what happened? Why didn't you—"

"We had a quarrel. I wouldn't forgive him when he asked me to. I meant to, after a while—but I was sulky and angry, and I wanted to punish him first. He never came back—the Blythes were all mighty independent. But I always felt—rather sorry. I've always kind of wished I'd forgiven him when I had the chance."

"So you've had a bit of romance in your life, too," said Anne softly.

"Yes, I suppose you might call it that. You wouldn't think so to look at me, would you? But you never can tell about people from their outsides. Everybody has forgot about me and John. I'd forgotten myself. But it all came back to me when I saw Gilbert last Sunday."

That got Anne to thinking, and the same afternoon she went to the schoolhouse where she knew Gilbert would be packing up his books for the summer.

"Gilbert," she said when she saw him. "Gilbert, I wish to apologize. I've been beastly for some time, and I think we should be friends."

Gilbert took her hand eagerly.

"Oh, Anne! Are we going to be friends? Have you really forgiven me my old fault?"

Anne laughed and tried unsuccessfully to withdraw her hand.

"I forgave you that day by the stream landing, although

70

I didn't know it. What a stubborn little goose I was. I've been—I may as well make a complete confession—I've been sorry ever since."

"We are going to be the best of friends," said Gilbert. "We were born to be good friends, Anne. You've thwarted destiny enough. I know we can help each other in many ways. We are kindred spirits, Anne! Come, I'm going to walk home with you."

Marilla looked curiously at Anne as she entered the kitchen later that afternoon.

"Who was that came up the lane with you, Anne?"

"Gilbert Blythe," answered Anne, blushing. "I met him at the schoolhouse."

"I didn't think you and Gilbert Blythe were such good friends that you'd stand for half an hour at the gate talking to him," said Marilla with a smile.

"We haven't been—we've been good enemies. But we have decided that it will be much more sensible to be good friends in the future. Were we really there half an hour? It seemed just a few minutes. But, you see, we have years' worth of conversations to catch up with, Marilla."

Anne sat long at her window that night. The wind purred softly in the cherry boughs, and the stars twinkled over the trees in the hollow.

She now knew that flowers of happiness would bloom

along her future path. Friendship and a rewarding career would be hers. And nothing could rob her of her ideal world of dreams.

"'God's in his heaven, all's right with the world,'" whispered Anne softly.